Magic
Animal Friends

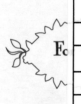

Special thanks to Valerie Wilding

ORCHARD BOOKS

First published in Great Britain in 2016 by The Watts Publishing Group

1 3 5 7 9 10 8 6 4 2

Text © Working Partners Ltd 2016
Illustrations © Orchard Books 2016

A CIP catalogue record for this book is available from the British Library.

ISBN 978 1 40834 110 0

Printed in Great Britain

The paper and board used in this book are made from wood from responsible sources

Orchard Books
An imprint of Hachette Children's Group
Part of The Watts Publishing Group Limited
Carmelite House, 50 Victoria Embankment, London EC4Y 0DZ

An Hachette UK Company
www.hachette.co.uk
www.hachettechildrens.co.uk

Lottie Littlestripe's Midnight Plan

Daisy Meadows

ORCHARD

Map of Friendship Forest

Can you keep a secret? I thought you could!

Then I'll tell you about an enchanted wood.

It lies through the door in the old oak tree,

Let's go there now - just follow me!

We'll find adventure that never ends,

And meet the Magic Animal Friends!

Love,
Goldie the Cat

Contents

CHAPTER ONE

Noisy Babies!

"I love the smell of fresh hay!" said Lily Hart, as she stuffed handfuls of it into a large wooden hutch. "This will make a lovely cosy bed for the baby badgers."

Lily and her best friend, Jess Forester, were inside Helping Paw Wildlife Hospital, which was in a converted barn

in the Harts' garden. Lily's parents ran
the hospital, and the girls helped out
whenever they could. They both adored
animals and loved caring for them.

Jess pushed the hay into place. "There!"
she said. "The little badgers will be comfy
in here."

"Let's hope they like it so much they

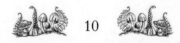

curl up to sleep," said Lily. "They're supposed to sleep during the day but they're so playful, they've been up all day and all night. They never stop!"

Jess watched the three little badgers chase each other, rolling over and over in a small pen nearby. She giggled. "I can see that!"

In a nearby hutch, a tabby kitten yawned. A tiny puppy in the pen opposite wriggled around and around, trying to get comfortable for his nap.

"Lots of the animals are sleepy this afternoon," said Lily.

She put on thick gloves and lifted the badgers, one by one, into the hutch. Their strong claws scrabbled about before they settled down and cuddled together.

"Now, try to sleep," Jess told them in a soothing voice. "Lily, let's put more hay in, to make it really snuggly."

She was just about to take some more

from the hay bale, when a beautiful golden cat with bright green eyes walked out from behind it.

"Goldie!" Jess and Lily cried.

The cat rubbed against their legs, purring loudly.

Lily's eyes sparkled. "She must have come to take us to Friendship Forest!"

Goldie was their special friend who took the girls on exciting adventures in Friendship Forest – a magical woodland world where the animals lived in little cottages and dens, and even on boats. But the best thing was that they could all talk!

Jess stroked Goldie's fur. "I wonder if Grizelda's causing trouble again," she said.

Grizelda was a horrible witch who wanted all the animals to leave Friendship Forest so she could have it for herself. Luckily, Goldie and the girls had always managed to save it from Grizelda's wicked magic.

"We'll soon find out," said Lily, as Goldie turned to leave. "Come on, let's follow her!"

Goldie led them towards Brightley Stream at the bottom of the garden, over the stepping stones and into Brightley Meadow. They raced across the grass towards an old, dead-looking tree in the middle of it.

The Friendship Tree!

Jess squeezed Lily's hand in excitement. As Goldie reached the tree, the bare branches sprouted fresh green leaves. Butterflies and starlings fluttered between the branches. In the grass below, bees buzzed happily among tiny pink flowers.

The girls stooped to read aloud the words written in the bark.

"Friend… ship… Forest!" A door with a leaf-shaped handle appeared in the tree trunk. Jess opened it, and golden light spilled out.

Lily and Jess held hands and followed Goldie into the shimmering glow. Their

 16

skin tingled all over, and they knew that they were shrinking, just a little.

As the light faded, Jess and Lily found themselves in a forest glade. The afternoon sun shone through the tall trees. The air was warm and smelled of delicious butterscotch.

And there was Goldie, now standing as tall as their shoulders and wearing her glittering scarf.

"Welcome back to Friendship Forest," she said in her soft voice.

The girls hugged her.

"It's great to be here!" said Lily.

 17

"And to talk to you!" said Jess. "Is Grizelda causing trouble with the Heart Trees again?"

Goldie shook her head. "No, we haven't seen her lately. The trees are safe at the moment."

The four Heart Trees were where the forest animals went when they needed help. The Memory Tree helped them remember what they'd forgotten, and the Laughter Tree helped them when they needed cheering up. The Sweet Dreams Tree and the Kindness Tree brought lots of happiness to the forest. But Grizelda was trying to ruin the Heart Trees. With the help of two young witches, Thistle and Nettle, she'd already put a spell on two of the Heart Trees – the Memory Tree and the Laughter Tree.

Lily, Jess and Goldie had managed to break the spells and repair the trees' hearts, but Grizelda still had two young witches left who could cause trouble: Ivy and Dandelion.

Lily smiled. "But if everything's OK, why did you fetch us?"

"It's a surprise!" said Goldie, her tail swishing happily. "Come on, let's go!"

She led the excited girls along a mossy path they'd never seen before. It wove between drifts of deep orange flowers that smelled of warm gingerbread.

Soon they emerged from the trees into a small clearing.

Both girls gasped in delight.

Pink, cream and yellow roses rambled and climbed among small trees around the clearing's edge. When they reached the top they wove together, making a flowery canopy.

"It's beautiful!" said Lily, looking up at the sweet-scented roses.

 20

"What's this?" asked Jess, walking under the canopy to look at a fence made of long, silky blue-green leaves. They were woven together to make a sort of house. Inside, laughing and playing, were lots of tiny animals.

Lily went to see, too. "Wow!" she said.

"It's a playpen for baby animals!"

CHAPTER TWO

The Fuzzle Nuzzle Nursery

In the pen were playful kittens, roly-poly puppies and lively little squirrels – there were baby animals of all shapes and sizes.

"They're so cute!" said Jess.

Above the pen, hammocks swung gently from rose-covered branches.

23

"Little beds!" said Lily.

Goldie smiled. "This is the Fuzzle Nuzzle Nursery." She waved to a young badger, who had a buttercup-yellow bow around her neck.

The badger ran over and threw herself at the girls, hugging them.

"This is Lottie Littlestripe," said Goldie. "Her family runs the nursery, so she helps look after the little ones. She's very excited to meet you."

"Hello, Lottie!"
said Jess and Lily.

"Hello! I've heard all about
you!" said the little badger. "And
I've got a surprise for you later!"
She clapped her paws excitedly.

"And here's Lottie's mum," said
Goldie, with a grin.

A smiling badger, wearing a
bright blue apron, came over. She
was cuddling a baby hare with very
long ears. A tiny fox cub peeped
out from her apron pocket.

"You must be Jess and Lily," she said.
"Welcome to the Fuzzle Nuzzle Nursery!"

"Ms Littlestripe runs the nursery, with
lots of help from Lottie," Goldie explained.
"It's where all the baby animals come to
play with their friends."

"Have a cuddle with Annabel, Jess," said

26

Ms Littlestripe, passing her the baby hare.
"And Lily, this is George." She took the
fox cub out from her apron pocket and
gave him to Lily.

George snuggled into Lily's arms.
"Want cuddles," he said, in a squeaky
baby voice.

"He's so sweet!" said Lily.

Ms Littlestripe laughed. "He's cheeky!"

"It must be—" Jess began, then she
laughed. Annabel the baby hare had
nuzzled against her neck – and her soft
fur was tickly. "It must be fun looking
after these cute baby animals!"

 27

"It is fun," said Ms Littlestripe, "but it's nap time for the little ones now."

"That's my job!" said Lottie.

Ms Littlestripe beamed. "Lottie can get any baby to sleep!"

"Do you sing to them?" asked Jess, stroking Annabel's silky ears.

"No, I make up bedtime stories," Lottie said. She smiled shyly. "I've made up a special one about your adventures in Friendship Forest. That's my surprise!"

Lily and Jess grinned at each other.

"Wow!" said Jess. "A story about us?"

"What a lovely treat!" said Lily.

George the fox cub stirred in her arms. "More cuddles!"

Ms Littlestripe laughed. "It's nap time, not cuddle time," she said. "Would you girls like to help tuck the babies into the hammocks?"

"Yes, please!" said Lily and Jess.

The squirrels all wanted to be together, so Jess tucked them in a hammock with soft mossy pillows, and put a cosy blue blanket across their middles.

Lily popped a tabby kitten, a baby otter, a mole and three mice in a second hammock. It wasn't easy keeping them

 29

settled, because the naughty mole kept burrowing under the blanket and tickling everyone's toes.

When the hammocks were full, the girls sat on the grass to listen to the story.

"Once upon a time," Lottie Littlestripe began, "there were two human girls. One had smooth dark hair. Her name was Lily. The other had curly fair hair, and she was called Jess. They—"

Lottie stopped

as the tabby kitten mewed crossly.
The otter was trying to get out of the
hammock, and was treading on the
kitten's tummy.

Other baby animals sat up and started
fussing noisily.

"Want to play!" said a squirrel.

"It's story time!" Lottie said. "Time
to rest!"

All the animals began
fidgeting and climbing
about in the hammocks.

"Oh, no!" whispered Jess. "None of the babies are listening to poor Lottie."

The little badger looked around and gave a sad sniff. "I don't understand," she said. "My bedtime stories always help them to sleep."

Ms Littlestripe looked worried. "They didn't have their nap yesterday, either," she said.

"I wanted everything to be perfect for the girls' visit," Lottie said tearfully. "But now it's all gone wrong."

She climbed onto Lily's lap and buried her face in her paws.

 32

"Don't worry," Jess said softly. "I'm sure we'll find a way to get them to sleep."

Goldie tapped her paw against her nose thoughtfully. "I've got an idea," she said. "Let's go to a Heart Tree for help. The Sweet Dreams Tree is where the animals go when they can't sleep. They pick a Dream Blossom and pop it under their pillow. That always makes them drop right off."

"But why aren't the baby animals sleeping?" Lily said anxiously. "Most babies love to— Oh!" she cried. "Perhaps Grizelda's done something to harm the Sweet Dreams Tree!"

"Like she did with the Memory Tree and the Laughter Tree?" Jess said in dismay. "We'd better find out!"

CHAPTER THREE

Dream Blossoms

Lily bent down and squeezed Lottie's shoulders. "Lottie, we must go to the Sweet Dreams Tree. We'll be as quick as we can."

The little badger grasped her hand. "Let me come and help," she begged. "Mum!" she called. "Please may I go?"

 35

Ms Littlestripe bustled over with her arms full of squirming otter babies.

"We'll look after her, we promise," said Lily.

Ms Littlestripe nodded. "Of course you can go. I'd like to come myself, but I have my paws full here."

"Wow!" cried Lottie. "This will be like being in a story!"

"Good luck!" her mum said. "I hope you find out why the babies won't sleep."

"We'll do our best," said Goldie.

Lottie, Jess and Lily followed her along a narrow mossy track, then onto a wide

path lined with purple flowers.

"This is the Heart Path," said Goldie.

The path was heart-shaped, and it linked all four Heart Trees. Lily and Jess knew it would lead them to the Sweet Dreams Tree.

Lily sniffed the purple flowers. "They smell like hot chocolate!" she said. "And they're bobbing in the breeze, as if they're nodding off to sleep!"

Goldie pointed to a small clearing just ahead. "That's where the Sweet Dreams Tree is."

But before they reached it, Goldie

stopped. "Stay quiet," she whispered.
"I think I heard someone nearby."

They peered between tall fern leaves.

"Wow!" Lily said softly. "What a gorgeous tree!"

The Sweet Dreams Tree had broad branches, with deep green leaves and large pink flowers. In the middle of the trunk was a hollow. Inside it, the tree's twinkling silver heart sat on a green mossy cushion. The girls knew that was the source of the tree's power.

"Those pink flowers are Dream Blossoms," whispered Goldie. "But there

 38

are usually lots
more of them. Something
is definitely wrong."

"They're beautiful," said
Lottie. "They look soft and
squashy, like candy floss!"

Jess gasped as a figure
with a puffball of yellow hair
appeared from behind the trunk.
"Dandelion!"

"Who is
Dandelion?" asked
Lottie, stretching up
her stripy nose to see.

"She's one of the young witches that have been helping Grizelda," Goldie said. "I bet she's up to something bad."

"She's picking a Dream Blossom," gasped Lily.

They watched as Dandelion held the flower against her cheek.

"Ooh, softy-wofty," they heard her say. "What shall I do with you?"

She tossed it into the air. It floated slowly down into her hands.

"I know!" she cried. "I'll turn you into a warty old toady-woady!"

She reached into her pocket and pulled

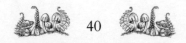

out lots of glass bottles.

"I remember, Dandelion loves potions."
Jess whispered.

Dandelion picked a dark blue bottle.
She removed the cork – *pop!* – and
muttered a spell as she sprinkled the
potion over the Dream Blossom. Stinky
yellow fog clouded around it. It cleared to
reveal a large spotty sock with a hole in
the toe.

Dandelion stamped her foot.

Goldie grinned. "That didn't work."

Jess, Lily and Lottie couldn't help
giggling quietly.

Suddenly a familiar figure strode into view – a tall woman with twisting locks of green hair and a thin, bony face. She was wearing a purple tunic over skinny black trousers, and high-heeled boots with pointed toes.

It was Grizelda the witch!

"We were right," Jess whispered. "She *has* done something to the tree! That's why the babies won't nap."

"Dandelion, fetch the last ingredient,"
Grizelda snapped.

"Ingredient for what?" wondered Lily,
as the yellow-haired witch reached into a
hollow in the Sweet Dreams Tree's trunk.

"Oh, no!" said Goldie. "Grizelda's
making a potion!"

She pointed to the edge of the clearing,
where a cauldron smoked and bubbled.

"We must stop her from
finishing it!" cried Jess.

As Dandelion pulled a
pillow made of greeny-gold
moss from the tree's hollow, the

four friends burst into the clearing.

"Stop!" Jess shouted.

"I've already got the last ingredient!"
Dandelion yelled at them. "So hard
lucky-wucky!"

"Don't give it to Grizelda!" Lily said.

The tall witch's mouth twisted into a
furious scowl. "You lot again!" she snarled.
"Here to ruin my spell? Well, you're too
late! I began this spell yesterday and the
magic is working already! Soon, no one
in Friendship Forest will be able to sleep!"
she shrieked. "They'll be exhausted. And if
they ever want to sleep again, they'll have

to leave MY forest – forever!"

"Get that moss, Jess," cried Lily, "so she can't finish her spell!"

Jess darted forward to snatch it from Dandelion, but Grizelda pointed a bony finger at the mossy pillow and it zoomed straight into her hands.

The witch screamed with laughter, held it high, then dropped it – *plop* – into the bubbling cauldron.

Swirls of grey fog climbed from the cauldron and snaked around the Sweet Dreams Tree.

Instantly, the last few Dream Blossoms

shrivelled and drifted to the ground. Then
something floated out of the hollow and
up into the air, twinkling silver through
the grey fog like a star.

Lily gasped. "The tree's heart!"

Grizelda clapped her bony hands
happily. "My spell worked!" she said. "The
heart's flying away where you interfering
girls can never reach it. Friendship Forest
will be mine!"

Her dark eyes glared into Jess and Lily's
faces. "And Dandelion's staying to make
sure you don't meddle with my spell,"
Grizelda snarled. "You'd better not let me

down like the other two," she snapped at
the young witch.

She clicked her fingers and suddenly
vanished, with her cauldron, in a burst of
smelly sparks.

Dandelion put her hands on her hips
and stuck out her tongue. "You silly
girly-wirlys! Give up and go away!"

She turned her back and picked up a
withered Dream Blossom. Then she pulled
another potion from her pocket. "Hmm,
what will this one do?"

Lottie's lip quivered as she watched the
young witch. "What are we going to do?

The babies will be so unhappy if they can't sleep." She buried her head in her paws.

Lily bent to comfort her. "Don't cry," she said. "We'll make everything all right, and you're going to help! It'll be a great adventure, won't it, Jess?"

But Jess didn't answer. She had spotted a silver light twinkling above the trees.

"It's the tree's heart!" she whispered. "Dandelion's busy with her potion, so let's follow it. Maybe we can get it back!"

CHAPTER FOUR

Midnight Market

Goldie, Lottie and the girls dashed
between trees, dodging around bushes as
they followed the twinkling light. But the
heart was always floating ahead of them,
just out of reach.

As they ran, the sun began to set and
the forest got darker. Lights gleamed in

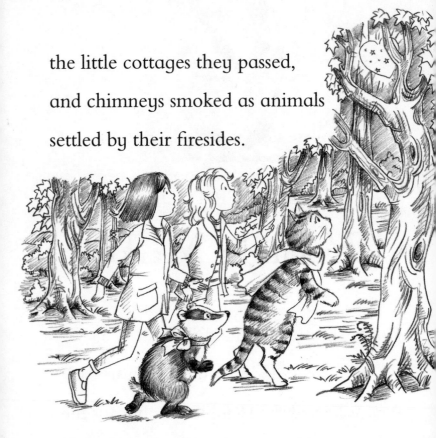

the little cottages they passed,
and chimneys smoked as animals
settled by their firesides.

As they ran through some chestnut
trees, the silver heart flew out of sight.
Lottie Littlestripe scanned the
darkening sky miserably. "It's gone!"

 50

Goldie stroked Lottie's cheek. "We're not giving up," she said.

"Of course not," said Jess. "But it's getting so dark. Thank goodness no time passes in our world while we're in Friendship Forest."

"Lottie's mum might be worried, though," said Goldie. "Let's send a flyer."

She crossed her paws and flapped them like wings. Moments later, a pink and gold butterfly fluttered down.

"Hello! I'm Popsy!" she said in a high, tinkling voice.

"Hello!" said Lily. She'd spoken to

 51

butterflies before, but it still gave her
a thrill to be able to call the beautiful
creatures.

Popsy settled on Jess's outstretched hand.

Lily said, "Please can you tell Ms
Littlestripe that Lottie will be out a bit
longer, but she's safe with us."

"Of course," said Popsy. She fluttered
down and perched on the tip

of the little
badger's
nose.
"Don't
worry,

Lottie," she said in her tinkling voice. "I'll tell your mum."

As the butterfly fluttered away, Lily heard a loud yawn.

"Listen!" she said.

There was another yawn. Then a big badger appeared from behind a moonflower bush. She carried a spade.

"It's my auntie, Mrs Stripyback," Lottie cried. "Hello, Auntie!"

"Hello, Lottie!" said the badger. "I've been digging tunnels all day and I'm worn out. But I can't sleep!" She yawned again. "I couldn't even take a nap."

She flopped down
against a tree trunk.
"I'm so tired. I just
wish I could sleep."

Jess glanced at
Lily. "I bet this is
because of
Grizelda's spell."

"Yes," said Lily.
"She said she started it yesterday.
That's why the animals couldn't sleep
then, either."

Lily gave a shout and pointed to a
twinkling light in the treetops ahead.

"Look! There's the heart!"

"We must go, Mrs Stripyback," Jess said. "You'll sleep soon, don't worry!"

"Follow me," called Lottie as she raced ahead. "Badgers can see just as well in the dark as we can in daylight!"

They raced past a group of holly trees, but then Goldie gave a groan.

"That's not the heart," she said. "It's the lanterns in the Midnight Market."

Lily's face fell, but then she brightened. "Lots of the other animals have gone home for the day now, but the Midnight Market's run by animals who come out at night. Let's ask if anyone's seen the heart."

Lily held Lottie's paw and they ran to the foot of the big oak tree that held the Midnight Market.

There was a wooden platform at the bottom of the tree. It had a fence around it, and a long vine hanging close by.

Goldie opened the gate and they piled in. Jess pulled the vine and the platform rose, up and up, until they could see above the smaller trees.

They stopped by a wooden walkway that stretched across the treetops. Tables stood along the sides, decorated with vines

and berries and lit by glow-worm lanterns.
Jess and Lily would have loved to stop and
look at the little scarves and seed necklaces
on display, and perhaps eat a star cookie
or moondrop cake, but there wasn't time.

The market was usually quite busy, but
tonight it seemed to be crammed with
animals, lots of them yawning because
they couldn't sleep.

"Melody Sweetsong!" Jess called to a
nightingale who was trying on a hat.
"Have you seen a twinkling light up in
the sky tonight?"

"Only stars," Melody trilled.

Shimmer Brightwing the firefly hadn't
seen any strange lights. Neither had Luna
and Dusky Longears the bats.

Lily spotted an elderly owl wearing a
waistcoat and monocle, and carrying a

 58

telescope. "It's Mr Cleverfeather!" she said. "Maybe he can help!"

She quickly explained to him what had happened. "Have you got an invention that could help us to find the heart?" she asked.

"Less, Yily," he said, muddling his words as usual. "Try my scellytope – I mean, telescope. I brought it because the Midnight Market's a good place for starwatching."

Lily peered through the telescope first, then Jess, then Goldie, but they had no luck spotting the flying heart.

 59

"Let me try," said Lottie.

Jess helped Lottie hold the telescope, hoping the little badger would see the heart with her night vision.

"I see it!" Lottie cried. "It's caught in the Twisty Willow Tree, quite close by! But it's not as bright as it was. If we go right now we might just catch it!"

"Great plan, Lottie!" said Lily. "Come on, everyone. Quickly – before Dandelion shows up!"

CHAPTER FIVE

The Twisty Willow Tree

Mr Cleverfeather opened his backpack and took out four thick wooden sticks, topped with giant fir cones.

"Take these to white your lay," he said, passing them round. "I mean, light your way! Blow on the cone."

 61

They all blew.

"Wow!" Lily cried in surprise, as
her cone shone with a warm golden
light. "Magical torches! Thanks, Mr
Cleverfeather!"

"You're welcome," he said, as they
started down the tree. "Be fair cool!"

Jess giggled as the platform lowered
them down. "He means be careful!"

When
they got to
the ground, Lottie led
the way through the trees.

When they reached the Twisty
Willow Tree, Jess and Lily saw it was
a tangle of knotted branches. Luckily,
the heart wasn't too high up.

"If you climb on my shoulders,

Lottie, I think you'll be able to reach it."
said Jess.

Jess and Lily lifted Lottie up and held
her legs as she pulled branches aside and
freed the heart.

"Well done!" said Goldie.

But the heart bobbed out of Lottie's
reach and floated higher up!

"It's floating away!" said Lily.

It bobbed further up and got caught
in the very top branches of a huge oak
tree. "We'll never reach it all the way up
there!" cried Lottie.

"It must be because of Grizelda's spell!"

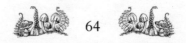

Jess said, as the girls lifted Lottie down. "She said it would fly away so we could never reach it. We must find a way to get that heart!"

"But how?" Lottie wailed.

Lily comforted her. "Don't worry," she said. "We know someone who'll help us – Great-Uncle Greybear!"

"Of course!" said Jess. "His scrapbook helped us break the spells Grizelda put on the other Heart Trees!"

"Then let's go!" Lottie cried.

"But what about the heart?" Goldie said. "What if it flies away again?"

"Don't worry, it's stuck!" Lily replied, pointing to where it was caught in one of the branches. "If we're quick, it'll still be there when we get back."

Great-Uncle Greybear's den was close by. When they reached the moss-covered door, they found it was open.

"That's odd," said Goldie, leading the way inside and downstairs, into the underground den.

Great-Uncle Greybear was dozing by the fire in his armchair, wearing comfy red pyjamas.

He jumped when he heard them.

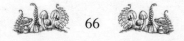

66

"Goodness!" he said. "Visitors!"

"Sorry, Great-Uncle Greybear," said Jess. "Did we wake you up?"

"No," replied the bear. "I keep trying to sleep, but I only doze. I can't seem to get to sleep at all at the moment." He smiled. "Do you young bears need to have a look in my scrapbook again?"

Jess and Lily nodded happily.

"Help yourselves," Great-Uncle Greybear said, getting up from his chair. "I think I'm going to get some hot cocoa from the Toadstool Café. Maybe that will help me nod off..." He padded out.

Jess went to the bookshelf, then turned to the others in alarm.

"The scrapbook's gone!" she whispered.

"It must be somewhere," said Lily.

They searched the whole room, but the book was nowhere to be seen.

Finally, they gave up and went back outside. At the top of the stairway Jess stopped suddenly, held up her torch and

peered through the
darkness.

"Dandelion!"

The small witch
was standing on a
broad tree branch, waving the scrapbook.

"I spied on
you!" she cackled.
"I heard about the
scrapbook. I'm so
clever-wever!"

"That's why
Great-Uncle
Greybear's door

was open," Lily said grimly.

Dandelion took a potion bottle from her pocket. "I'll turn this book into a lump of mould," she giggled. "Lovely mouldy-wouldy!"

"Don't!" Goldie cried.

Dandelion uncorked the bottle, held it over the scrapbook and chanted:

"Potion, change this book I hold,

Turn the pages into—"

"GOLD!" shouted Lottie.

Dandelion dropped the book in shock.

Lily darted forward and grabbed it. The pages gleamed golden in her torchlight.

The young witch screeched with rage and jumped down from the branch. "Give that back!"

Lily held it behind her back. "No way!" she shouted.

"Go away!" yelled Jess.

Dandelion huffed and stamped her foot. "You'll be sorry!" she screeched. "Now I'll make a potion that does something really bad!" Then she poked out her tongue and stormed off.

Lily opened the book. "It's golden but we can still read it!" she cried. "Lottie, you're so clever! How did you think of an ending for the spell so quickly?"

Jess grinned. "Because she's used to making up stories with brilliant endings!"

The little badger couldn't stop smiling as Lily turned the gold-coloured pages.

"Here!" she cried. "This might help! It's a diary entry Great-Uncle Greybear wrote about the Sweet Dreams Tree when he was little."

Jess shone her torch on it and read out loud:

"Today, naughty Zachary Clawfoot the crow stole the mossy cushion from under the Sweet Dreams Tree's heart to line his nest, and the

 72

tree's heart floated away! It wouldn't come back until it had a new mossy pillow of Slumber Moss to rest on."

"That's it!" cried Goldie. "We need to make a new pillow out of Slumber Moss. Then the heart will come back."

Lottie bounced excitedly. "We use Slumber Moss to make pillows for the Fuzzle Nuzzle babies!" she cried. "It grows on the far side of Willowtree River."

Lily scooped Lottie up and hugged her. "What would we do without you?"

"There's one problem," said Jess. "Dandelion might have already seen this!

 73

She might be after the moss!"

"You're right!" said Lily. "We must find the Slumber Moss before she does. Dandelion's spells keep going wrong, but the next one might just work!"

CHAPTER SIX

Slumber Moss

Goldie, Lottie and the girls slithered down
a slope covered with pink feather grass,
giggling as it tickled their ankles.

"Faster," cried Goldie. "We must get the
Slumber Moss before Dandelion does!"

When they reached the riverbank,
everyone was relieved to find that

Dandelion was nowhere around.

Lily raised her torch and peered across the water. Here and there, on the far riverbank, were glowing greeny-gold patches.

"There's the Slumber Moss!" she cried.

"Great!" said Jess. "But how can we cross the river?"

Goldie pointed to a pretty blue and yellow barge bobbing gently by the bank. "That's where the Featherbill duck family lives. I bet they can take us across."

The four friends made their way along the water's edge, through tall bulrushes.

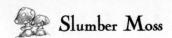

The reflections of their torches gleamed like gold in the water.

"There's Ellie Featherbill," said Lottie, as they reached the barge and saw the little duckling sitting in a deck chair.

She waved hello.

"Oh, no, can't you sleep either, Ellie?" said Goldie. "You must be tired."

"Very tired," said Ellie, "but I still can't sleep, so I'm watching the moon."

"Please could you take us across the river in your barge?" Jess asked.

But Ellie shook her head and said sleepily, "We tried to take the barge up the river this afternoon, but everyone was too tired to get it moving."

Lily looked at Jess in alarm. "We must find some way to get across."

Before they had time to think, there was a *crack!* and Dandelion appeared in a shower of sparks.

"No, you don't!" she said. "I've got a fantastic new potion!"

Dandelion pulled out a glass bottle and sloshed the contents into the river.

"Ha!" she crowed. "My Go Fast Potion will make the river far too fast for anyone to get across!"

Lottie clutched Jess's hand.

"Don't worry," said Jess. "That potion probably won't work, either."

"But it *is* working!" cried Lily.

They watched, horrified, as the water
ran faster and faster. Soon it surged past
in a torrent.

"Ha!" cackled Dandelion. "Now you'll
never get that mossy-wossy!"

She clicked her fingers and vanished in
a spatter of sparks.

There was a loud creak from the
Featherbills' barge.

"Quick!" cried Jess. "The barge is moving. Grab the ropes!"

Goldie and the girls dived for the ropes that dangled over the barge's side. They pulled them, digging their heels into the

ground to stop the barge being swept downriver.

"Let's tie it to that tree," panted Jess.

When the barge was safe, the girls

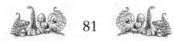

turned to comfort Lottie. But she was lying down on her tummy, peering over the edge of the riverbank.

"Lottie, are you OK?" Lily cried.

But when Lottie scrambled back up, she was smiling!

"Look what the barge was sitting in front of," she said.

Jess and Lily peered over the edge of the bank where the barge had been. There were three steps dug into the earth that led to a big hole.

"It's a tunnel!" cried Jess in amazement.

"It's Auntie Silverback's," said Lottie.

"I remember her saying she'd dug a tunnel that goes under the river. We can get across now!"

"Hooray!" cried Goldie. "Let's go!"

The little badger hurried down the steps and disappeared into the tunnel. Goldie followed. The girls peered after them as their fluffy tails disappeared down the tunnel.

Jess gave Lily a worried look. The tunnel was even darker than the forest.

"Come on," Lily said encouragingly. "We've got torches."

They crawled inside.

"It smells nice," said Lily. "Like fresh earth after the rain."

"Or potatoes before they've been scrubbed," said Jess.

When they emerged on the far bank, they were relieved to see that the raging river was already starting to slow down.

"Phew!" said Jess. "Dandelion's potion couldn't stop us after all."

"Hey, girls!" came Goldie's voice. "Quick! Over here!"

The girls turned to see Lottie and Goldie beside a patch of greeny-gold moss. Both animals had their arms full.

"We've got the moss!" Jess cheered.

She and Lily stuffed moss into their

pockets and up their

sleeves, then followed

Lottie and Goldie

back along the

tunnel.

They climbed

out carefully, in

case Dandelion was

nearby. The water

was calm again, and

the only sound was the whistling of the

wind in the reeds.

 85

"Let's make the pillow," said Lily, pulling moss from her sleeves.

They worked together, patting and pushing the Slumber Moss into a pillow.

Jess held it to her cheek. "It's so soft, I could go to sleep right now."

Lily laughed. "Not yet! We still need to get the heart down from the treetop!"

Lottie grinned. "That's right – the story isn't over. We still need to make sure there's a happy ending!"

CHAPTER SEVEN

Lottie's Special Story

Jess carried the pillow as the four friends
raced through the forest, back towards the
Twisty Willow Tree.

"I hope the heart's still stuck in that
oak tree," Jess panted.

They passed many tired animals.
Captain Ace the stork was leaning

wearily against
the basket of his
hot-air balloon.
Melody Sweetsong the
nightingale was trying
to sing a soothing night-time tune to all
her sleepy neighbours.

"No one can get to sleep," Goldie said.

"We'd better hurry," said Lily.

Suddenly Lottie yelped, "I see it!"

The heart was floating in the same spot
between the branches of the oak tree. It
was barely twinkling at all.

Jess stretched as high as she could,

 88

holding up the mossy pillow.

For a moment, nothing happened. Then the heart drifted slowly, slowly down, and settled onto the pillow of Slumber Moss.

"Hooray!" everyone cried.

"We've got the heart," said Lily.

"Now back to the Sweet Dreams Tree," said Goldie.

It wasn't far. Jess and Lily breathed sighs of relief as the tree loomed out of the darkness. But they stopped in fright as a figure stepped out from behind the trunk.

Dandelion!

When she saw what Jess was holding,

the small witch stamped her foot. "Not fair!" she said. "You've got the heart and I'm too tired to make more potions. I'm so crossy-wossy!"

To Jess and Lily's dismay, Dandelion began to sob.

Lottie went over and reached up a paw to pat her hand. "Don't cry," she said. "I get grumpy when I don't get enough sleep, too! Would you like a special bedtime story? It's called… 'Dandelion's Perfect Potion'!"

The witch sniffed. "Yes, please," she said.

They sat down, and Lottie began:

"Once upon a time, there was a witch with beautiful yellow hair. One day…"

Jess, Lily and Goldie left Lottie telling her story and carefully placed the cushion and the heart into the tree.

The heart glowed silver, then began to sparkle, brighter than before.

"It's like starlight!" said Lily.

"And the magic's working again," said Goldie. "Look at the tree!"

All at once the pink Dream Blossoms bloomed along its branches, bursting into flower like popcorn in a pan.

"Beautiful!" said Jess.

Lottie glanced over and gave a big grin.

She continued telling Dandelion her story.

But just then a yellow-green orb

zoomed across the clearing, and with a

cra-ack, Grizelda appeared. Her bony

face was crimson with fury and the locks of her green hair crackled and whipped around her face.

"You meddling girls ruined my plan!" she screeched. "But I'm not finished with you! Dandelion will make a new potion that will ruin the forest!"

Lottie giggled.

Grizelda glared at the little badger. "What are you laughing at, stripy?"

Lottie pointed to Dandelion.

Jess laughed, too. "She's fast asleep!"

"It doesn't look as if Dandelion's going to make anything, Grizelda!" said Lily.

The witch scowled. "I'll be back," she snarled. "You'll pay for this!"

She snapped her fingers, vanishing in a shower of sparks that left a very nasty smell in the air.

The four friends looked at one another, then at the sleeping Dandelion.

"Hooray!" they whispered.

CHAPTER EIGHT

Sleep at Last!

Goldie, Lottie and the girls left Dandelion
sleeping, and carried armfuls of Dream
Blossoms to the Fuzzle Nuzzle Nursery.

On the way, Jess yawned. "The blossom
magic's working on me!" she said.

"And me," Lily and Goldie said.

"Ooh!" said Lottie. "Why not have a

sleepover with me?"

Jess and Lily nodded in delight.

"We'd love to," said Jess, "but only if you tell us the bedtime story you wrote!"

Lottie clapped her paws. "I'd nearly forgotten!" she cried. "Of course!"

The nursery was quiet when the friends arrived. They crept inside the fence to find the hammocks full of babies, all fast asleep. The only sounds were snuffles and gruffles, snores and sighs.

"Aren't they sweet?" whispered Lily, peering at some baby bunnies.

Ms Littlestripe woke up, and climbed out of her hammock. When she heard how clever and brave Lottie had been, she hugged the little badger.

"I'm so proud of you," said Ms Littlestripe. "The babies and I decided to have a sleepover while we waited."

Lottie piled the Dream Blossoms in a box. "We'll keep these for whenever the babies have trouble sleeping," she said. Then she showed Goldie and the girls a big spotty hammock.

"Can we sleep here, Mum?" she asked.

The girls, Lottie and Goldie snuggled under a cosy blanket in their hammock.

"Story time!" said Lily.

Lottie smiled. "Once upon a time," she began, "there were two girls."

"And a cat!" added Lily.

"And a badger!" chimed Jess.

Lottie smiled. "Yes, that's right!"

Jess snuggled into Lily, who snuggled into Lottie, who snuggled into Goldie.

"And together, the four of them went on a great adventure…"

They closed their eyes and drifted off…

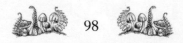

The next morning, the girls woke to the sound of baby animals playing happily.

Ms Littlestripe bustled over with a tray in her paws and a row of baby bunnies tucked into her apron pocket.

"Crispy toast with sunberry and hazelnut spread," she said, "and raspberry smoothies."

"Thank you!" the four friends said.

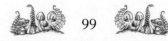

They climbed out of the hammock
and sat on the grass to eat. Several baby
animals came to share their breakfast!

"That was the best sleep ever, but
Lily and I must go home now," said Jess.
"Lottie, thanks for our bedtime story!"

The little badger smiled shyly. "Thanks
for letting me come on your adventure,"
she said. "It was like being in my very
own story!"

As the girls stood up, a nearby
hammock moved and a face peered over
the edge.

"Dandelion!" said Jess.

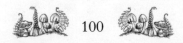

Ms Littlestripe smiled. "She arrived just after you all fell asleep. I think she followed you. She just tumbled into the hammock and started snoring!"

"Dandelion, you'd better not be planning any trouble," said Goldie.

The witch shook her head. "I'm not. I feel better after a nice snoozy-woozy," she said. "Can I stay in the forest like the other witches and guard the Sweet Dreams Tree? I'll make sure Grizelda doesn't harm it."

"That's a great idea!" said Jess.

"We'll see you next time we visit the forest," added Lily.

Before the girls left, Lottie gave them each a Dream Blossom. "If ever you can't sleep," she said, "this will help."

When everyone had hugged and said goodbye, Goldie and the girls left the Fuzzle Nuzzle Nursery and headed for the Friendship Tree.

"Thanks for your help," Goldie said when they reached it. She touched a paw to the trunk and a door appeared.

"Be sure to fetch us if Grizelda tries any

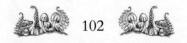

more tricks," said Jess. "After all, there's still one Heart Tree left that she hasn't attacked yet."

"I will!" Goldie said, hugging them.

The girls stepped through the door into the shimmering glow. Immediately, they felt the tingle that meant they were returning to their normal size.

When they stepped out into Brightley Meadow, it was still afternoon. They held hands and ran back to Helping Paw Hospital.

"I've got a great idea!" said Lily. "We can use the Dream Blossoms here too!"

She opened the hutch door and tucked the Dream Blossoms into the hay bedding.

The badgers sniffed. They stopped wrestling and squealing and went to curl up beside the flowers. A hush fell over the barn as the other tired animals settled down to nap as well.

Jess grinned. "Brilliant! Now they can all catch up on their sleep."

"And they didn't even need a bedtime story!" Lily smiled.

The End

Nasty witch Grizelda has used her bad magic on the Kindness Tree, and now all the animals keep being mean! Can Jess, Lily and baby owl Matilda Fluffwing fix the last Heart Tree?

Find out in the next adventure,

Matilda Fluffywing Helps Out

Turn over for a sneak peek . . .

At last Goldie stopped by a strange round building, like a huge nest, up in a tree. It was made of many branches woven together, each covered with bright blue and yellow flowers.

A sign above the door said, 'Get Well Grove.'

"The Fluffywing family live here," Goldie explained. "Mr and Mrs Fluffywing are both doctors. They care for all the forest animals."

She jingled the feather-shaped doorbell.

They heard an excited squawk, and a door above them burst open.

Out fluttered a little white owl, wearing a purple and green striped bobble hat.

"You must be Jess and Lily!" the owl cried. "I'm glad you've come."

"Yes we are," Lily smiled. "What's your name?"

"Matilda Fluffywing," said the owl, hovering in front of them.

Read

Matilda Fluffywing Helps Out

to find out what happens next!

Magic
Animal Friends

Can Jess and Lily stop Grizelda and her young witches from ruining the Heart Trees? Read all the books in series four to find out!

www.**magicanimalfriends**.com

Puzzle Fun!

Oh, no! Lottie Littlestripe is lost in her sett!
Can you help her find her way back out?

Lily and Jess love lots of different animals –
both in Friendship Forest
and in the real world.

Here are their top facts about

BADGERS

like Lottie Littlestripe:

• A female badger is known as a 'sow' and a male badger is known as a 'boar'.

• With their sharp claws and strong legs, badgers are fantastic diggers.

• Badgers are nocturnal animals, but they have very bad eyesight. Luckily, they have fantastic hearing and a very good sense of smell.

• Badgers live in underground houses called 'setts'.

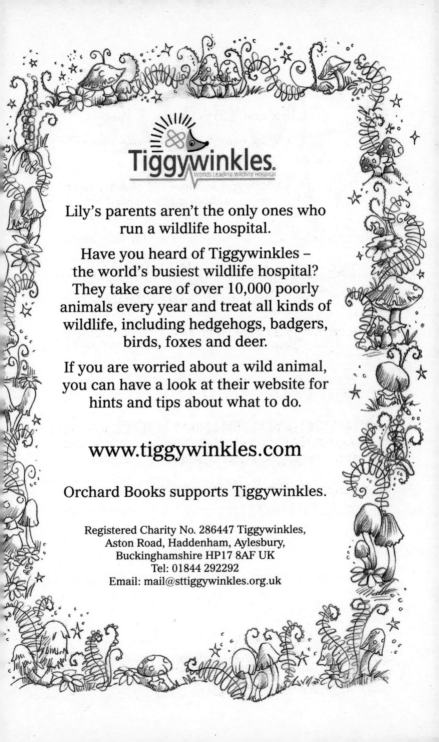

Tiggywinkles.
World's Leading Wildlife Hospital

Lily's parents aren't the only ones who run a wildlife hospital.

Have you heard of Tiggywinkles – the world's busiest wildlife hospital? They take care of over 10,000 poorly animals every year and treat all kinds of wildlife, including hedgehogs, badgers, birds, foxes and deer.

If you are worried about a wild animal, you can have a look at their website for hints and tips about what to do.

www.tiggywinkles.com

Orchard Books supports Tiggywinkles.

Registered Charity No. 286447 Tiggywinkles,
Aston Road, Haddenham, Aylesbury,
Buckinghamshire HP17 8AF UK
Tel: 01844 292292
Email: mail@sttiggywinkles.org.uk

Magic Animal Friends

Can you keep the secret?

There's lots of fun for everyone at
www.magicanimalfriends.com

Play games and explore the secret world of
Friendship Forest, where animals can talk!

Join the
Magic Animal Friends Club!

Special competitions

Exclusive content

All the latest Magic Animal Friends news!

To join the Club, simply go to

www.magicanimalfriends.com/join-our-club/